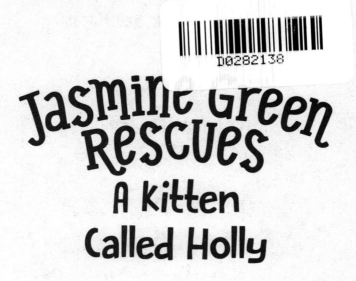

Jasmine Green Rescues
A Kitten Called Holly

Helen Peters
illustrated by Ellie Snowdon

WALKER BOOKS

For Jimmy, Patrick, and Megan
HP

For my sister, Lizzie
ES

Text copyright © 2017 by Helen Peters
Illustrations copyright © 2017 by Ellie Snowdon

First US edition 2020
First published by Nosy Crow (UK) 2017

Library of Congress Catalog Card Number pending
ISBN 978-1-5362-1027-9 (hardcover)
ISBN 978-1-5362-1572-4 (paperback)

20 21 22 23 24 25 TRC 10 9 8 7 6 5 4 3 2 1

Printed in Eagan, MN, USA

This book was typeset in Bembo.
The illustrations were done in pencil with a digital wash overlay.

Walker Books US
a division of
Candlewick Press
99 Dover Street
Somerville, Massachusetts 02144

www.walkerbooksus.com

Read all the books in the
Jasmine Green Rescues series

A Piglet Called Truffle
A Duckling Called Button
A Collie Called Sky
A Kitten Called Holly
A Lamb Called Lucky
A Goat Called Willow

Oak Tree Farm

Truffle found this way

Willow found this way

To village and school

Tom's house

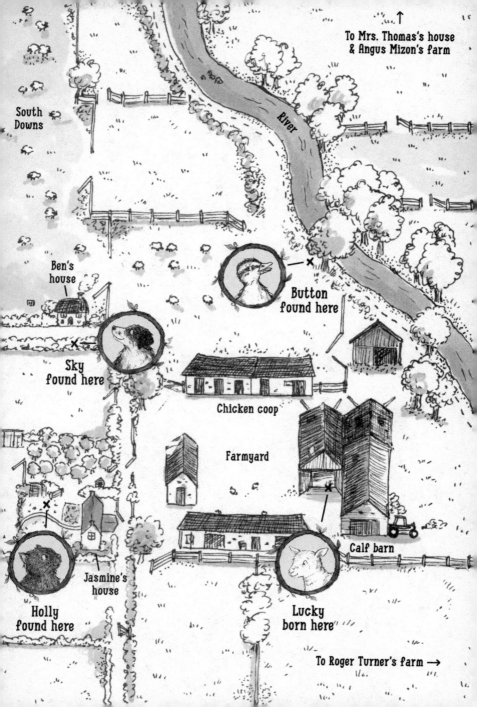

To Mrs. Thomas's house
& Angus Mizon's farm

River

South
Downs

Ben's
house

Button
found here

Sky
found here

Chicken coop

Farmyard

Calf barn

Holly
found here

Jasmine's
house

Lucky
born here

To Roger Turner's farm →

1
It Sounds Really Fierce

"This is perfect," said Jasmine, smiling at her best friend, Tom. "Come in, Sky, and don't make a sound. We have to keep it secret from Manu."

Jasmine's collie, Sky, wagged his tail and padded into the shed. Jasmine pulled the door shut. It was coming off its hinges, and the rotting wood dragged along the ground. It clearly hadn't been shut properly for years.

"Sit, Sky," said Jasmine, and Sky obediently sat on the dusty floor.

"I can't believe we've never been in here

before," said Tom. "It will be really cozy when we've cleaned it up. Look, it's even got a window."

"We can bring out some old chairs," said Jasmine, "and find something for a table. And we can clear all the junk out."

The shed was a small brick building with a sloping roof in the garden of the farmhouse where Jasmine lived. Two rusting oil stoves stood in one corner, next to a tangled bundle of wire and a collapsed straw bale. On a rough wooden shelf sat a couple of dusty old jam jars containing screws and nails.

"Look," said Tom, "there's a mouse skeleton on the floor. Manu would love that for his collection."

"We can give it to him as a present," said Jasmine. Her six-year-old brother, Manu, kept a gruesome collection of animal bones and skulls in his bedroom. "But we won't tell him where we got it. This clubhouse is our secret."

"That shelf will be perfect for books," said Tom.

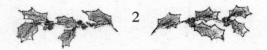

"And we can put our maps of the rescue center up on the wall."

It was a Friday afternoon in late October, and they had a two-week fall break stretching out in front of them. Jasmine and Tom were planning to run an animal rescue center when they grew up, and their new clubhouse was where they were going to work out all the details.

"What should we call the club?" asked Jasmine.

"The Animal Rescue Club," said Tom.

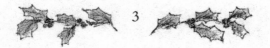

Jasmine screwed up her nose. "Not very original." Then her eyes lit up. "Oh, but it's A.R.C. for short! I think Mom told me about a rescue organization in Kolkata with those letters, too. Arc. Like Noah's Ark."

"Exactly," said Tom. "So it's where abandoned animals come to be safe. Like you, Sky."

He reached down to stroke Sky's silky fur, and Sky wagged his feathery tail across the floor.

Three months ago, Jasmine had found Sky abandoned and left to die in a hedge. She had nursed him back to health and now he was completely devoted to her. Jasmine and Tom had also rescued a clutch of orphaned duck eggs from the riverbank in the spring, after a dog had killed the mother duck. The surviving duckling, Button, was now a full-grown drake who lived happily with the free-range chickens. And Jasmine's very first rescue animal had been a tiny runt piglet that she had found on a neighboring farm. She had called the piglet Truffle, and the sick little runt

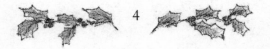

had turned into a giant sow who lived in the orchard behind the farmhouse.

"I'm not allowed to keep any more animals," said Jasmine. "Mom and Dad made me promise that if I rescue any more, I have to rehome them."

"Will you still be able to look after my guinea pigs at Christmas?" asked Tom.

"Of course I will," said Jasmine. "Are you going to your granny's in Cornwall again?"

"Yes," said Tom. "It's going to be great. She makes the best Christmas dinner ever. And we're going to swim in the sea on Christmas morning."

"Swim in the *sea*? On Christmas Day?" said Jasmine. "Why?"

Tom was about to reply when something thudded against the door. Then came frantic scratching on the wood and an ear-piercing yowl.

The children looked at each other in alarm.

"Sounds like a cat," whispered Jasmine.

"A really angry cat," said Tom.

"Maybe it's a wild cat," said Jasmine, "and it's been living in this shed. And now we've shut the door and it can't get in."

The cat continued to yowl and scratch at the door.

"We could tame it and have it as our club mascot," said Tom. "If it's living here, it kind of belongs to the club anyway."

"That's a great idea," said Jasmine. "And I wouldn't be keeping an animal, because this is its home already."

"I wonder what it looks like," said Tom.

They tried to peer through the cracks in the door, but the gaps were too narrow and they couldn't see the cat.

"We need to let it in," said Jasmine, "if it lives here."

"We'd better stand far back," said Tom.

"I don't think it will hurt us. It's probably just confused because the door's shut."

Tom looked doubtful. "I don't know. It sounds really fierce."

6

"It'll be fine," said Jasmine confidently. She pushed the door open.

A shrieking bundle of gray fur shot into the shed. It hurled itself at Jasmine, hissing and spitting. She screamed and covered her face with her hands as the cat leaped up at her, scratching and biting. Jasmine screeched in pain. With a final terrific yowl, the cat sprang down and bolted out of the shed.

"Are you all right?" asked Tom, sounding shaken.

Jasmine sat heavily on the collapsing bale behind her. She looked at her hands. They had deep, red scratches all along them.

"That must really hurt," said Tom.

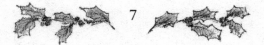

Jasmine clutched her hands together to try to stop the pain. "That cat really didn't want us to be here. Ow, my hands sting so much."

"You need to run them under the tap," said Tom. "Let's go inside."

Jasmine frowned. "What was that?"

"What?"

"That funny squeaking sound."

"I didn't hear anything."

"Listen," said Jasmine.

They listened. Birds tweeted in the garden. Sheep baaed in the field. From the orchard came Truffle's low, contented grunt.

"I can't hear anything," said Tom. "Let's go."

They stepped out into the sunny garden, avoiding the prickly leaves of the holly bush beside the shed. Then Jasmine heard it again: a high-pitched sound, somewhere between squeaking and mewing.

She turned to Tom. His expression showed her that he had heard it, too.

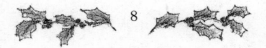

"What is it?" he whispered.

"I don't know," said Jasmine, "but there's something in there."

They crept back into the half-light of the shed. There was another squeaking sound.

"It's coming from behind that bale," said Tom.

The baler twine that had held the straw together had broken, so much of the straw had collapsed in a messy heap. The children peered over the bale into the dark corner.

Jasmine gasped in delight. "Kittens!" she whispered. "Oh, they're so cute!"

"Three of them," said Tom, grinning with excitement. "They're tiny."

The kittens were cuddled up in a deep nest of straw. One was a tabby, one was orange, and the third was black. The tabby kitten and the orange one lay still, but the black kitten was crawling over its littermates, mewing.

"They're gorgeous," said Jasmine. "I wonder how old they are."

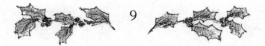

9

"They can't be newborn," said Tom, "because their eyes are open."

"So they must be at least a week old. I don't think they're much older than that. They're so little."

The black kitten gave another piercing mew.

"It wants its mother," said Tom. And then he drew in his breath and looked at Jasmine in horror.

"Oh, no," said Jasmine. "That cat. She must be their mother."

"We shut her out from her kittens," said Tom. "And now we've frightened her away."

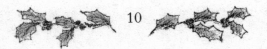

2
What If She Doesn't Come Back?

"That's why she was so fierce," said Jasmine. "She thought we were threatening her babies."

"We need to get her back," said Tom. "If she can't feed the kittens, they'll die."

They walked out into the garden, looking for the cat. But there was no sign of her.

"How are we going to get her back?" asked Tom. "She's completely wild. She's not going to come if we call her, is she?"

Jasmine thought for a second. Then she said,

"Food. All animals come for food. And she must be really hungry if she's feeding kittens."

They ran up the walkway and in through the back door of the farmhouse to the mudroom. Jasmine had two cats of her own, Toffee and Marmite, and their food was kept in the cupboard next to the sink. She grabbed two pouches from the box and some empty takeout containers from the next cupboard.

"We'll use these as bowls," she said. "We can lay a trail of food across the garden, leading up to the shed. That should tempt her back."

In the garden, Jasmine tore the top off the first pouch and started squeezing it into a container.

"Don't put too much in each one," said Tom, "or she'll be full before she gets to the shed."

They put a little food in each container and laid them in a line from the bottom of the garden to the shed. Then they tiptoed in to look at the kittens. The black kitten was still mewing piteously.

"Do you think we should give them some milk?" asked Tom.

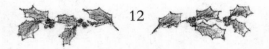

"Kittens can't have cows' milk," said Jasmine. "It upsets their stomachs. I wish Mom or Dad were here. They'd know what to do."

Jasmine's dad was a farmer and her mom was a vet. Dad was out in the fields feeding his calves, and Mom was working at the vet's office.

"You could phone the office," said Tom. "Even if your mom can't speak to you, one of the nurses would know what to do, wouldn't they?"

"Good idea," said Jasmine. "Let's do that now."

"Should I stay here," Tom asked, "and keep an eye on the kittens?"

"They should be OK for a bit. And the mother won't come back if we're here. We should leave them alone so she feels safe to return."

"Hopefully she'll smell the food," said Tom, "and she won't be able to resist."

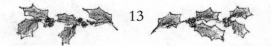

"What did Linda say?" asked Tom when Jasmine put the phone down. Linda was the head nurse at Mom's office.

"Well, we need to take away the food bowls near the shed," said Jasmine. "Come on."

"Why?" asked Tom as they ran down the walkway.

"She said it's good to leave food out, but it should be at least three yards from the nest. The mother won't go back to the kittens if there's food nearby because she won't want to attract other cats to her nest."

Tom picked up the food bowl in the shed. "And what about the kittens?" he asked.

Jasmine took the bowl they had left outside the door. "Linda said we should leave them. Their mother has to go off hunting, so they're used to being alone for short periods. And they can survive for several hours as long as they're warm and dry."

Tom looked worried. "But the mother was probably coming back from hunting when we scared her away. She might have been out for hours already."

Jasmine stared at him anxiously. "I hadn't thought of that."

"So what should we do?" asked Tom.

"I don't know. We definitely shouldn't touch them. The mother won't like it if there's a strange scent on them. Linda said the mother might move them anyway now, since we've disturbed her nesting place." Jasmine looked at Tom and saw that he felt as guilty as she did.

"But what if she doesn't come back?" asked Tom. "They won't survive on their own for much longer."

"Linda said we should watch from a distance to see if she comes. Let's get a blanket and wait on the other side of the garden."

"And if she doesn't come?" asked Tom.

"I don't know. But I'm sure she will. They're her babies, after all. She's bound to come back."

Jasmine tried to sound confident, but inside she felt horribly worried. What if the mother cat never returned?

Then she and Tom would be responsible for orphaning three tiny kittens, not to mention causing terrible distress to the poor mother.

They grabbed a blanket from the cupboard under the stairs and sat by the hedge on the other side of the garden. They waited for what seemed like hours. As dusk fell, the colors of the garden faded and the world began to turn to shades of gray.

"I'm freezing," Jasmine whispered.

"Me, too," said Tom. "I wish I had gloves."

Jasmine thought about going inside to fetch

gloves and a warmer coat, but she was afraid to move in case the cat was nearby and she accidentally frightened her away again.

Why wasn't Mom home from work yet? Jasmine checked her watch and was amazed to find that only twenty-five minutes had passed since they had sat down.

Then Tom nudged her. "Look," he whispered.

Slinking silently through the shadows by the hedge was the mother cat. She slipped inside the shed.

Jasmine felt her shoulders drop with relief, and realized that she must have been hunching them all this time.

"Phew," said Tom. "I was so worried. Those poor kittens must be so hungry. I bet they're pleased to see her." He stood up and rubbed his hands together. "I'm freezing. Let's go in."

But Jasmine was still watching the shed. "Wait," she said.

"Why?"

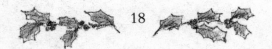

"Remember what Linda said? The mother might take them away."

Tom frowned. "She wouldn't really, would she?"

But he turned to look at the shed. And at that moment, the cat came padding out through the doorway, carrying a kitten in her mouth.

"Oh, no," said Jasmine. "She *is* moving them."

"We should follow her," murmured Tom. "See where she goes. Come on."

Jasmine grabbed the hem of his coat. "No," she whispered. "We might scare her even farther away. And she might not come back for the others if she knows we're nearby. Let's just watch from here."

Tom sat down. They watched the cat as she slunk back along the hedgerow. Near the bottom of the garden, she disappeared behind a bush. They kept looking but she didn't reappear.

"She went through the hedge into the fields," said Tom. "She might be going miles away."

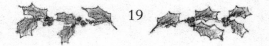

"She's got to come back for the other two, though," said Jasmine.

"How about when she comes back for the next one, we just creep down the garden on this side?" said Tom. "She won't see us from over there, and we might find out where she's going."

So when the cat padded back a few minutes later and fetched the second kitten, Tom and Jasmine stood up very quietly and crept down their side of the garden, keeping pace with her. When she disappeared behind the bush again, they moved slightly farther down, so they would see her come out on the other side.

The cat emerged from behind the bush and padded on toward the bottom of the garden, the kitten dangling from her mouth by the scruff of

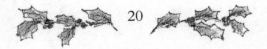

its neck. When she reached the hedge, she didn't take her kitten through it, as they had feared she would. Instead, she headed for the rickety old wooden toolshed in the far corner of the garden. The door was shut, but there was a gap at the bottom of the wall where one of the planks had rotted away. The cat squeezed through the gap and disappeared into the shed.

Jasmine grinned at Tom. "That's perfect!" she whispered. "She's stayed in the garden!"

Tom looked excited. "We can leave food out for her, and then she'll grow tame, and we'll be able to play with the kittens."

"Jasmine, Tom, are you out there?" called Jasmine's mom from the top of the garden.

"Quick," whispered Jasmine, "before she shouts again and scares the cat away."

"There you are," said Mom as they ran up the path. "What are you doing out here without coats on? You must be frozen. Come in for dinner. It's all ready."

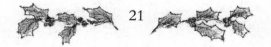

"We have to stay out a little bit longer," said Jasmine. "It's an emergency." And she quickly told her mother the whole story.

"Well, it sounds as though everything's fine," said Mom. "The cat's moving her kittens to a safe place."

"But she hasn't moved the third kitten yet. We need to make sure she comes back for it."

"There's no reason to suppose she won't," said Mom. "You can check after dinner. Dad made spaghetti Bolognese."

The mention of her favorite dinner reminded Jasmine how cold and hungry she was. She and Tom followed Mom up the path.

"We'll come out right afterward," said Jasmine, "and make sure she's taken the third kitten."

"And if she has," said Tom, "we can start cleaning up the clubhouse tomorrow."

"Two whole weeks of vacation," said Jasmine. "We can make the clubhouse amazing."

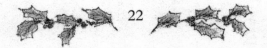

3
We Can't Let It Die

In the farmhouse kitchen, Dad was serving dinner. Manu and his best friend, Ben, were sitting at the table, sucking spaghetti noisily into their mouths. Jasmine's sixteen-year-old sister, Ella, was also there, a book propped open in front of her.

"How was your school trip, boys?" asked Mom. Manu's class had spent the day at a local museum, learning about King Charles II.

Manu grinned. "It was so cool," he said. "We

saw a dead fox on the road. It was all squashed in the middle where a car had run over it."

"Ugh," said Jasmine. "That's disgusting."

"And what about the museum?" asked Mom.

"Lunch was really good," said Manu. "Noah didn't like his sandwich, so we swapped, and his mom uses this really soft white bread that you can squish into balls and throw at people. You should buy that kind of bread, Mom."

"So what did you learn about King Charles the Second?" asked Dad.

Both boys looked blank. "What?"

"King Charles the Second. Isn't that who you were supposed to be learning about?"

"Oh, we didn't really listen to that part," said Manu. "We were playing with this bit of play-dough Ben found in his pocket."

"Everyone was sitting on the floor cross-legged," said Ben, "and we were sticking little blobs of playdough on the bottom of people's shoes in front of us. So when they stood up, their

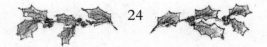

shoes were all sticky on the floor and they didn't know why. It was so funny."

"Great," said Dad. "Excellent. Time well spent, then."

"What if the kitten's still there when we go back?" asked Jasmine.

Ella looked up from her book. "What kitten?"

"We found a nest of kittens," Jasmine said.

"Where?" asked Manu, an excited gleam in his eyes.

Tom shot Jasmine a warning look.

"Just in the farmyard," said Jasmine vaguely. "In one of the buildings. Anyway, the cat's moved them now."

"But you said a kitten might still be there," said Manu.

"Mom said the mother would have come back and gotten it," said Jasmine.

"Me and Ben will find them," said Manu.

"No, you can't!" said Jasmine in alarm. "If you disturb them, the cat will move them again."

25

Jasmine ate her dinner as quickly as she could. As soon as Tom put the last of his spaghetti in his mouth, she said, "Please may we leave the table?"

"Where are you going?" asked Manu.

"Just up to my room."

She and Tom left the kitchen. But they didn't go upstairs. Instead, Jasmine grabbed a flashlight from the hall cupboard while Tom opened the front door as quietly as he could. Then they crept out into the dark garden.

They didn't expect to find anything in their clubhouse. The mother cat had had plenty of time to collect the third kitten. But as they drew near to the shed, they heard a high-pitched mewing.

"Oh, no," said Jasmine. "She hasn't come back."

They tiptoed inside. Jasmine shone the flashlight to one side of the nest so as not to frighten the kitten by shining a light directly into its eyes.

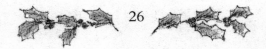

There, all alone, was the little black kitten. It was clearly distressed, crawling around in the straw, mewing urgently and continuously. Tears sprang to Jasmine's eyes as she watched it.

"We have to take it to its mother," she said.

"We can't," said Tom. "You said if she finds our scent on it, she'll reject it."

"But look at it. It will die soon if it doesn't get fed."

"We should leave," said Tom. "She might be coming back right now."

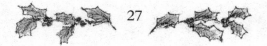

"I don't think she's going to come," said Jasmine. "She collected the second one right after the first, didn't she? Why has she left this one so long?"

Tom was silent for a minute. Then he said, "Let's ask your mom what we should do."

Jasmine leaned over and spoke to the kitten. "We'll be back in a minute, little one. We're going to find out how to help you."

To their relief, Manu and Ben had left the kitchen by the time they got there. Mom and Dad

were clearing the table. When Jasmine explained the situation, Mom looked thoughtful.

"I'm afraid it sounds as though the mother has rejected this one," she said. "Was it mewing when you first saw them?"

"Yes," said Tom. "The other two were lying there peacefully, but the black one was crawling around and mewing."

"Hmm," said Mom. "So the mother had probably already rejected it. If the other two were quiet and content, they were probably well-fed, but it sounds as though the black one was already hungry."

"Should we take it to the mother?" asked Jasmine.

Mom shook her head. "No. If you take back the one she's rejected, she might reject the others, too."

"So what should we do?" asked Jasmine. "If we leave it, it will die."

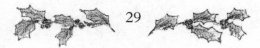

Mom and Dad exchanged a look. Jasmine glanced at Tom and saw her own excitement mirrored in his face.

"We can't let it die, can we?" said Tom.

Dad looked at Tom and then at Jasmine. "Clearly this kitten needs to be looked after," he said. "So I guess you'd better bring it indoors."

"Calm down, you two," said Mom as Tom and Jasmine shrieked with excitement. "You can bring the kitten in and look after it, but we're not having any more pets, Jasmine. You already have two cats, two dogs, a pig, and a duck. As soon as the kitten's old enough, we're going to

find a home for it. Do you
understand?"

Jasmine looked despondent.
But she said, "Yes, I understand."

"And you promise me you
won't beg and pester to
keep it?"

"I promise. Come on, Tom, let's
go and get our new kitten!"

As they ran down the garden path, Jasmine turned to Tom. "I know I can't keep the kitten," she said, "but you could."

"I wish I could," said Tom, "but Mom hates animals in the house. She only let me have the guinea pigs because they live outside. There's no way she'd let me have a cat. I've asked her a bunch of times, but she'll never change her mind."

4
We're Going to Look After You

The black kitten was mewing more piteously
than ever when the children got back to the shed.
Tom held the flashlight while Jasmine reached
down and gently scooped up the tiny animal. It
looked at her with its enormous blue eyes and
mewed desperately.

"It hardly weighs anything," she said, stroking
the kitten's silky-soft fur.

Tom cupped his hands. "Can I hold it?"

Jasmine set the tiny kitten in Tom's hands. "I

wonder if it's a boy or a girl," she said. "Mom will be able to tell."

"Hello, little kitten," said Tom. "You're so lovely."

"It's starving," said Jasmine. "Come on. We need to give it milk."

"I thought you said they couldn't have milk," Tom said as they hurried back to the house.

"Not cows' milk. It probably needs a special kitten formula. I hope Mom's got some in the car."

The trunk of Mom's car was always crammed with boxes of equipment and medicine for treating sick animals. As Jasmine and Tom got back to the kitchen, Mom came in through the other door, holding a plastic container with a picture of a cat on one side.

"Oh, great," said Jasmine, grabbing the tub. "You've got kitten milk."

"Calm down, Jasmine," said Mom. "There's no need to snatch."

"But it's an emergency. The kitten's starving."

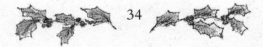

Mom smiled at the mewling kitten. "What a sweet little thing."

Jasmine scanned the writing on the container, looking for instructions on how to prepare the formula.

"It's so cute," said Tom, stroking the kitten. "Why would the mom reject it?"

"I was going to talk to you both about that," said Mom as Jasmine opened the tub and took out the measuring scoop. "I know it's impossible not to get attached to a beautiful kitten, but the problem is that nature often does know best."

Jasmine didn't like the sound of that. "What do you mean?"

"I mean that when a cat rejects her kitten, she often does it for a reason. This kitten might not be completely healthy. It might have something wrong with it that isn't obvious yet. I just want you to be prepared, that's all."

"Prepared for what?" asked Jasmine. "Are you saying the kitten might die?"

As Mom started to reply, her work phone rang. She pulled it from her pocket and walked into the hall to answer it.

Jasmine was used to conversations ending abruptly every time Mom's phone rang. It always meant an animal emergency of some kind, and if Mom was on call, she had to drop everything and go.

"Sorry, you two," Mom said when she reappeared. "I've got to go and see a horse over at Selham. Use a syringe to feed the kitten—very slowly, just a few drops at a time, because if the milk goes in too fast, it could go into the windpipe. I'll get you a proper feeding bottle tomorrow. Dad's in his office if you need anything."

Jasmine was measuring the powdered milk into a jam jar. "Could you just tell us if the kitten's a boy or a girl?" she asked.

Mom examined the kitten. "She's a girl," she said. "And you're very beautiful, aren't you?"

She smiled at the kitten and handed her back

to Tom. "Keep her warm," she said. "That's really important. And make sure she's sitting up when you feed her. Now I've got to run." She kissed the top of Jasmine's head, grabbed her car keys, and left.

Jasmine held the measuring scoop under the faucet. "Two parts water to one part formula," she said. She tipped two scoops of water into the jar, screwed on the lid, and shook it hard. "That's a lot, but we can keep the rest in the fridge and warm up a bit for each feeding."

Tom was studying the side of the formula tub. "We need to weigh her," he said. "It says you have to feed them eight cc per ounce of weight every twenty-four hours. How much is eight cc?"

"It should say on the syringe," said Jasmine. "I'll go and get one."

When she returned from the mudroom with a plastic syringe, the little kitten was sitting in the kitchen scale pan, her blue eyes huge and frightened.

"Six ounces," said Tom. He lifted her out and held her against his sweater. "After we've fed her, I'll make an actual chart, and we can write down her weight and how much she eats every day, like we did with Sky."

He took a note-pad and pencil from the drawer. "So eight cc per ounce of weight means eight times six. How often does it say we should feed her?"

Jasmine consulted the side of the tub. "Every three hours."

"Through the night as well?"

"I guess so," said Jasmine. "We'll have to set the alarm." Tom was staying for a sleepover.

"Or we could just stay awake all night," said Tom.

Jasmine smiled. "That's a much better idea." She unscrewed the lid of the jar and swirled the milk around to check for lumps. "How much should we give her?"

"Six cc per feed," said Tom, who had worked it out on the notepad.

Jasmine dipped the syringe into the jar and drew up the plunger. She pushed back her sweater sleeve and dropped a little milk onto her wrist to check that it was at body temperature.

"Perfect," she said. "You're going to be fed now, little kitten."

She pushed the plunger down to the six cc mark. "Do you want to feed her?" she asked Tom.

"You should do it," said Tom. "I got to hold her all this time. I'll read about looking after her."

Jasmine sat down and Tom passed the mewing kitten to her. Jasmine moved her finger to the kitten's mouth to pry it open, but there was no need. The kitten opened her mouth and started to suck at her finger. Jasmine took the

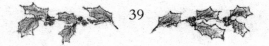

syringe and carefully dropped a little milk into her mouth.

The kitten moved her head around and batted at the syringe with her front paws. Jasmine used her free hand to keep the paws away as she tried to keep the syringe in the kitten's mouth and not spill the milk. It was hard to move the plunger slowly enough to only release a drop or two at a time.

"It will be much easier once we have a bottle," she said to Tom when he returned with Mom's laptop. "But at least she's drinking. That's a good sign."

"What should we call her?" asked Tom.

"You should name her," said Jasmine. "I named Sky and Button and Truffle."

Tom narrowed his eyes thoughtfully. "Hmm." He was silent for a minute and then he said, "Holly. I like that name. And there's a holly bush right outside the shed where we found her."

"Holly," said Jasmine. "That suits her." She looked into the kitten's blue eyes. "Hello, Holly. We're going to look after you."

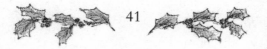

5

She'll Change Her Mind in the End

Manu came into the kitchen while Jasmine was giving Holly the last of her milk and Tom was reading advice online about looking after orphaned kittens.

"Are there any cookies?" Manu asked. Then he saw Holly and his eyes lit up. "Oh, he's so cute! Can I hold him?"

"She's a girl," said Jasmine, "and she's called Holly. You can hold her when she's finished feeding."

"It says we need to burp her when she's finished," said Tom. "Like a baby."

"I remember Mom doing that with Manu,"
said Jasmine. "You hold them over your shoulder
and rub their back. It gets out the trapped air."
She turned to her brother. "I hope Holly's not
like you. You used to throw up after every single
feeding."

"Do you have a shoebox?" Tom asked. "It says
a shoebox lined with a towel is the best bed. And
she needs a heating pad."

Jasmine frowned. "I don't think we've got one
of those."

"Or you can use a hot water bottle. But that
might be a bit big. She needs to be able to move
away from it if she gets too hot."

"What about that mini hot water bottle you
gave Dad last Christmas?" suggested Manu.
"The one he puts in his coat pocket for a hand
warmer?"

Jasmine looked at her brother in amazement.

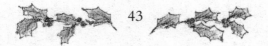

"That might be the first useful thing you've ever said."

Manu looked wounded. "I say useful things all the time. You just don't listen."

Jasmine handed Holly to Tom and rummaged in Dad's coat pockets for the mini hot water bottle.

"Actually, instead of a towel, we should use a blanket from the cats' basket," said Tom, still reading the website. "So that Holly will get used to Toffee and Marmite's scent."

"Manu!" shouted Ella from upstairs. "Why is the bathroom sink full of bones?"

Manu went to the doorway. "I was washing them," he shouted back.

"Well, come and get them out."

"In a bit," said Manu.

"Now!" shouted Ella.

Manu gave a heavy sigh and left the room.

"Here it is," said Jasmine, pulling the hot water

bottle from one of Dad's coat pockets. She put
the kettle on and went to fetch a shoebox.

When she returned, Tom whispered, "Look,
she's sleeping."

Jasmine looked. Holly was snuggled up in Tom's
lap, her eyes closed, looking perfectly contented.

"She's so gorgeous," said Jasmine.

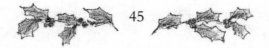

Tom scratched the back of his hand. "I've got bites," he said. "They're really itchy."

Jasmine looked at the little red marks and made a face. "Oh, dear," she said. "I think you've got fleas."

Tom looked horrified. "Fleas?"

"They must be from Holly," said Jasmine. "Never mind. We'll comb them out."

Tom was frantically scratching his arms. "Oh, no, I'm itchy all over now. My mom will freak out if I have fleas."

Jasmine grabbed the flea comb from the mud-room. She knelt beside Tom and ran it through Holly's fur. Holly opened her eyes sleepily and closed them again.

"Sorry, Holly," said Jasmine, "but I'm going to have to comb every part of you. You just keep on sleeping."

"It did say on that website that you have to check feral cats for fleas," said Tom, "but Holly

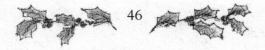

46

looked so clean and silky that I didn't think she'd have any."

"You can never tell," said Jasmine. "Fleas are so small, you hardly ever see them."

"What's a feral cat anyway?" asked Tom. "Does it just mean a wild cat?"

"I think wild cats are a whole different species," said Jasmine, "and feral cats are just normal cats that don't have homes."

She wiped the comb on a piece of paper towel. There were a few flecks of black on the white paper. Jasmine held the paper under the tap and dripped water onto it. The black specks turned dark red. "Yep," she said. "Flea dirt. It's actually dried blood, you see. Holly's blood, poor thing."

She combed the underside of Holly's tail and then inspected the comb. "And there's a flea."

She crushed the flea in the paper. "You have to be really vicious with them," she said. "They're so tough, they can survive almost anything."

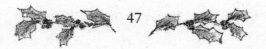

"My mom definitely won't let me have her now," said Tom. "Not once she sees I've got flea-bites."

"Don't let her see, then."

"She'll notice. She notices everything."

"But we can't let Holly go to another home," said Jasmine. "You'll have to convince your mom."

"I'll really try," Tom said. "I'll tell her there's nothing else I want for Christmas."

"That might work," said Jasmine. "Holly won't even cost anything. And if your mom won't budge, I'll persuade mine to let me keep her."

But when Mom came home, she wasn't in a persuadable mood. She wouldn't even let Jasmine and Tom set an alarm to give Holly a night feed.

"She's nearly two weeks old, by the look of her," Mom said, "and she doesn't need feeding in the middle of the night. You can give her a late feed tonight, and you can get up early, but you're not setting your alarm for two a.m."

"OK," said Jasmine.

48

We'll just have to stay awake all night instead, she thought.

Mom looked at her suspiciously. "And if I hear a sound out of you after I've switched off your light, Holly will be going to a shelter in the morning."

Jasmine stared at her mother in horror. "You wouldn't do that!"

"Try me," said Mom. "I'm not having two exhausted children in the house tomorrow. If you want to look after her, you'll need your sleep."

"OK," said Jasmine again. But she had every intention of staying up all night. And Mom clearly didn't trust her, because she insisted on leaving Jasmine's bedroom door open after she had switched out the light, and then she went into her study next to Jasmine's room and left that door open, too.

Tom and Jasmine lay silently in their sleeping bags, with Holly curled up in her shoebox on the floor between them, fast asleep with a tummy

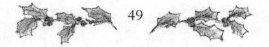

full of milk. They listened for the sound of Mom leaving her study, planning to get up as soon as she went downstairs. But Mom just carried on tapping at her computer. Maybe she was writing an email to Jasmine's nani in Kolkata. Was she ever going to stop?

6
So Lucky We Found Her

Jasmine was woken by a little mewing noise. Her heart leaped with excitement. Holly!

It was pitch-dark. She pressed the light button on her alarm clock.

6:36 a.m.

Oh, no! They hadn't woken at two o'clock. Holly would be starving. They were terrible kitten owners.

Jasmine slipped out of bed. She could just see the shoebox in the shadows. She put her hand gently inside it and her fingers touched the kitten's soft, warm fur. Holly gave another squeaky meow. Jasmine stroked her and picked up the box. "I'm so sorry, Holly," she whispered. "I'm going to feed you right now."

As she was tiptoeing out of the room, she heard Tom stir. She turned.

"Jasmine?" he said sleepily.

Holly mewed again. Tom sat bolt upright.

"I'm going to feed her," said Jasmine.

"Wait, I'm coming," said Tom, scrambling out of his sleeping bag.

They padded down to the kitchen. Jasmine fetched the milk and warmed it up.

"Can I feed her?" asked Tom, lifting Holly out of her box. She was mewing continuously now.

"She's so hungry," said Jasmine. "I hope she wasn't mewing for ages before I woke up." She tested the milk on her wrist. "OK, this is the right temperature."

"Look," said Tom. "She's sucking my finger."

It didn't take long for Holly to drink her milk. Tom burped her and then held her up to his face.

"All kittens are born with blue eyes," he said. "I read that last night. It said they start changing color in a month. I wonder what color Holly's will be."

"Maybe they'll stay blue," said Jasmine. She raised her finger a few inches in front of Holly's face and slowly moved it in a circle. Holly looked at it for a few seconds, and then she batted a tiny paw at it. Tom and Jasmine laughed.

"She's playing with us already!" said Jasmine. "That's a great sign."

Tom scratched the red bites on his hand. "We'd better flea-comb her again once she goes to sleep. And that won't be long. The website said kittens sleep for twenty hours a day."

Sure enough, a few minutes later, Holly fell asleep in Tom's lap. Jasmine went to get the flea comb. Toffee and Marmite looked up from their bed on the counter as she came into the mudroom. Toffee jumped to the floor and rubbed himself against Jasmine's legs.

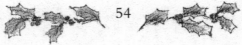

Tom and Jasmine had just read about introducing older cats to a new kitten. Before introducing them, you were supposed to get them used to each other's scents, as a cat's sense of smell is its most important sense for communication.

"Sorry you can't go in my room at the moment," said Jasmine as she stroked Toffee's orange fur. "Once you get to know Holly, you can go wherever you like again, but we need to take it slowly."

Toffee nuzzled at her hand, investigating the new scent.

"That's Holly you smell," Jasmine told him. "We'll introduce you to her soon. I'm going to swap your blankets so you'll get used to each other's scents. And remember, even though we have a new kitten, I still love you just as much as I always did, and I'll give you just as much attention as I always have."

After they had combed Holly and put her back in Jasmine's room, Jasmine said, "We should go and see if the other kittens are OK."

"But what if we disturb them," said Tom, "and the mother moves them again?"

"We'll tiptoe up really quietly and peep in the shed window. I just want to make sure they're all right. What if she's rejected them, too?"

That settled it. They put on coats and boots and went out to the garden. To their relief, the cat and her two remaining kittens were nestled in a heap of empty paper sacks.

"They look so cute," said Tom. "Do you think they'll be OK? It's horrible to think what hard lives they might have, living in the wild."

"We won't let that happen," said Jasmine. "We're going to bring them indoors."

Tom stared at her. "Your mom will never let you."

"We have to persuade her," said Jasmine. "We'll make a plan. After all, she's a vet. She can't want to see animals suffering in her own backyard."

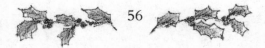

When they went into the kitchen for breakfast, Mom was making scrambled eggs. Ella was sitting

at the table, highlighting passages in her book. Tom and Jasmine sat opposite her.

"Morning, you two," said Mom. "How's Holly? I gather you've fed her, from the mess you left on the draining board."

"Sorry," said Jasmine. "I'll clean it up. She seems fine. Do you really think there's something wrong with her?"

"Don't worry, Jasmine," said Mom. "If she's eating well and she seems all right, I expect she'll be fine. I'll give her a full examination this morning anyway."

"It was so lucky we found her, wasn't it, Tom?" said Jasmine, giving Tom a meaningful look. This was his cue to put their plan into action.

"Yes," said Tom. "Otherwise she'd have died. Eighty percent of feral kittens die in their first year."

Ella looked up from her book, her eyes wide with alarm. "Eighty percent?" she said. "Why?"

"Accidents or disease, usually," said Jasmine. "We've been reading about it. And the females

58

can become pregnant at four months old if they're not rescued. And then they're pregnant or rearing kittens their whole lives. It's so hard for them, and they can get terrible diseases."

"And they abandon their kittens, and then the kittens starve," said Tom. "It's awful."

"It is," said Mom. "That continual breeding cycle is no good at all. As soon as the kittens are weaned, we'll catch them in a humane trap and I'll neuter them and the cat. Then they'll have much healthier lives."

"And then can we bring them inside and tame them?" asked Jasmine.

Mom gave her a hard stare. "Jasmine, I've already told you we can't. This house is chaotic enough without two more feral kittens."

"We're not asking to keep them forever. Only until they're tamed and old enough to go to new homes."

"I know it's hard to understand," said Mom, "but cats that haven't had human contact in their

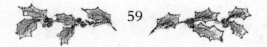

first few weeks of life are actually much happier living outdoors, as long as they have food and shelter. These ones are in an ideal situation. They can sleep in the shed, they'll have the whole farm to roam around, and you can put food and water out if you want to. Put it somewhere quiet and out of the way—under a bush or something. And do it in the daytime, not at night, so you don't get nocturnal wildlife taking it."

"But what if the kittens like us," said Jasmine, "and they want to be pets?"

"Jasmine, I've said you can rear Holly and you can feed the others. I think that's quite enough, don't you?"

Jasmine decided not to push her mother any further right now. She would have to bide her time.

After breakfast, Mom gave Holly a full health check. She examined her all over, took her temperature, and then listened to Holly's heartbeat through her stethoscope.

"Is she all right?" asked Jasmine anxiously when Mom unhooked the stethoscope.

"As far as I can tell, she's absolutely fine. Clear eyes and nose, normal temperature, and a good strong heartbeat."

"But you said her mother had probably rejected her for a reason."

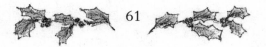

"It might have been any one of a number of reasons, though," said Mom. "We'll probably never know. It might have been something to do with the mother, not Holly. I can't be certain that Holly is fully well, because there might be a problem with one of her organs that hasn't shown up yet. But she certainly seems to be a healthy little kitten. And very beautiful, too, aren't you, Holly?"

She put out her finger and Holly batted it with her tiny paw.

"She's the cutest kitten ever," said Tom. "I wish I could have her."

"Ask your mom when you get home," said Jasmine.

"I will. But she won't let me; I know she won't. She hates cats."

"She couldn't possibly hate Holly," said Jasmine. "Nobody could."

Tom went home an hour later. That afternoon, he phoned Jasmine.

"Mom saw the fleabites," he said. "She got so upset. There's no way she'll let me have Holly now."

"But Holly won't have fleas when you take her home."

"I told her that, but she wouldn't budge. It's not just the fleas. She went on and on about how

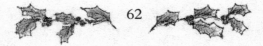

cats scratch the furniture and leave hairs everywhere and bring dead animals into the house. She said cats are dirty, nasty creatures and there was no way she was having one in her home. I haven't spoken to her since."

If Tom's mom was going to be so horrible about cats, Jasmine thought, then there was no way she was ever going to have Tom's mom in *her* home. How dare she call them dirty, nasty creatures!

"Well," she said, "if your parents really aren't going to change their minds, I'll just have to persuade mine."

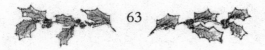

7
School Is So Annoying

It was the first Monday of November, the day school started again after fall break. Mom was stirring a pan of porridge on the big Aga stove. Ella sat at the kitchen table with a cup of tea, a book lying open in front of her as usual. Jasmine was kneeling on the floor, playing with Holly.

At four weeks old, Holly was much steadier on her feet and wonderfully playful. Jasmine pushed a toy mouse across the tiles to her. Holly jumped on it and started to bite it with her tiny new teeth. Jasmine pulled the toy away and Holly leaped on it again, nuzzling and nipping at its fur.

"It's so unfair that we have to go back to school just as Holly's getting really playful," said Jasmine. "She'll be so lonely all day without me."

Jasmine and Tom had turned Sky's puppy crate into a playpen for Holly, where she would spend the days while Jasmine was at school. The wire crate had a fleecy blanket on the floor, a sleeping hammock, a box that Holly liked to hide in, a water bottle, and her scratching post and litter tray. Jasmine had also put some of Holly's favorite

toys in there, including toilet paper tubes and Ping-Pong balls, which she loved to chase.

"She'll be fine," Mom said. "She'll play for a while, and then she'll curl up and sleep, and you can lavish attention on her when you get home. She'll be able to see the other cats, so she won't be lonely. And Dad's going to check on her regularly, isn't he?"

"But it's not the same as me being there," said Jasmine. "If we could bring the other kittens in when they're weaned, she'd have companions all the time."

Mom gave her a warning look. "Don't even start, Jas."

The mudroom door rattled as Dad came in from the farmyard. Jasmine heard him taking off his boots and washing his hands. He walked into the kitchen and warmed his hands at the Aga.

"Chilly out there," he said. "Wouldn't be surprised if we have frost tomorrow."

Mom served the porridge into bowls. Jasmine

sat at the table and sprinkled hers with sugar.

Holly padded over and started batting at her pant hems. Jasmine took a fluffy toy mouse on a string out of her pocket and dangled it in front of Holly. The kitten jumped up on her hind legs and grabbed the mouse in her front paws.

"You're so clever, aren't you?" said Jasmine, bending down to stroke her. "You're the cleverest kitten in the whole wide world."

Mom looked up as Manu walked into the kitchen, still in his pajamas.

"Oh, Manu, go and get dressed," she said. "And hurry up, or your porridge will be cold."

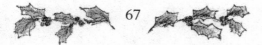

Manu was in the doorway when he suddenly stopped.

"Oops," he said.

"What?" asked Mom.

"I just remembered. I have to go to school dressed as Samuel Pepys."

"What?" said Mom and Dad together.

"Yes, we're doing the Great Fire of London and I'm Samuel Pepys, that Parliament guy who kept a really detailed diary."

"But that's ridiculous," said Mom. "We would've gotten a letter if you had to dress up today. They'd have given us some warning, at least."

Manu looked sheepish. "There might have been a letter."

"Where is it?" asked Mom in her sternest voice.

Manu took his book bag from one

of the coat pegs on the wall, rummaged through its contents, and eventually produced a crumpled paper airplane. He handed it to Mom. She unfolded it, read the letter, and sat down heavily.

"Oh, dear lord, the local paper's coming to photograph the whole first-grade class in their seventeenth-century costumes this morning. Manu, how could you have forgotten to mention this the entire vacation?"

"He'll just have to go in a trash bag," said Dad. "I'm sure Samuel Pepys wore something black and shiny."

"He can't go in a trash bag again," said Mom. "You'll have to do something, Michael. I need to be at the office in half an hour."

"I'd love to," said Dad, "but I've got someone coming to deliver the new calf feeders, remember?"

The doorbell rang. "That must be them," said Dad. "Sorry, must get going." He practically sprinted out the door.

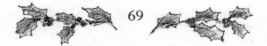

Mom put her head in her hands. "I can't believe you've gotten me into this, Manu. What on earth am I going to do?"

"I'll make him a costume," said Ella.

They all stared at Ella. She held out her phone, on which was a picture of an old-fashioned man in a long curly wig and a shirt with ruffles under a brown jacket.

"That's him," said Manu excitedly. "That's Samuel Pepys!"

"I'll need your black leggings, Jas," said Ella, "and your white knee-length socks to go over them. I'll make some buckles out of foil for Manu's shoes."

"But you'll be late for school," said Mom.

"I'll only miss homeroom," said Ella. "It'll be fine."

Jasmine was studying the picture. "He can wear his normal uniform shirt," she said, "and we can tear up some strips of sheets from the rag bag to be the ruffles."

"If we put a belt around Mom's brown jacket," said Ella, "that will be perfect."

"And he can have that wig from the dress-up box," said Jasmine. "I'll style it a bit."

Mom was staring at her daughters in wonder. "You're angels, you really are. I'm eternally grateful to you. Just remember to put Holly in her playpen before you leave, won't you, Jas?"

Jasmine picked Holly up. "Look at her beautiful little face," she said to Mom. "She hasn't been any trouble, has she?"

"She's been very good," said Mom. "Where are my car keys?"

Jasmine fetched them from the dresser. "And she gets along fine with the other cats, doesn't she?"

"Thanks," said Mom, taking the keys. "Yes, they seem to have settled down well together."

"So it wouldn't be any trouble to keep her, would it?"

Jasmine fixed her mother with what she hoped was a soulful gaze.

"An extra animal always means more work," said Mom. "Not to mention more expense."

"But she's so lovely," said Jasmine. "Who would want to get rid of such a beautiful little kitten? You don't really want to let her go, do you?"

Mom sighed. "Jasmine, you promised not to pester. And this really isn't the time to discuss it. I have to go to work, and you have to make a costume and go to school."

Jasmine sighed. "School is so annoying. Six whole hours in the same room as Bella Bradley. Ugh."

Jasmine and Manu arrived at school just as everyone was filing into the building. Manu, resplendent in wig and ruffles, made his way to his classroom. Jasmine's classmates were hanging up their coats outside their classroom. There was lots of chatting going on, but Bella Bradley's voice could be heard above everybody else's.

"What are you getting for Christmas?" she asked her friend Sadie. "My parents said I could get a new pet."

"You're so lucky," Sadie said with a sigh. "You've already got a dog."

"Rupert's not all mine, though," said Bella. "He belongs to the whole family."

Jasmine and Tom exchanged glances. Bella's dog, Rupert, had killed Button's mother as she was sitting on her nest last spring. Bella had been letting him run free among Jasmine's dad's sheep.

"I can't choose between a puppy and a kitten," said Bella. "I've been researching, and I've seen

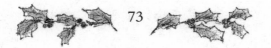

the cutest little cat collars and cat beds, and these gorgeous matching feeding bowls."

"Why don't you get a kitten, then?" asked Sadie.

"Yes, but if I get a puppy, you can buy the most amazing coats for them, and if you get one of those tiny ones, you can carry it around in a special puppy handbag. I wish I could get both. It's not fair."

"Ugh," said Jasmine to Tom as they walked into the classroom. "I can't believe she's getting a pet and all she cares about is what accessories she can buy for it."

"She shouldn't even be allowed to have a pet," said Tom, "after letting her dog kill Button's mother."

"If I ever meet her parents," said Jasmine, "I'll tell them how irresponsible they are."

"I don't suppose your mom has changed her mind about you bringing the other kittens indoors?" asked Tom.

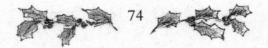

"Nope. Has your mom changed her mind about you having Holly?"

"No," said Tom gloomily. "I've tried and tried, but she won't budge."

"Why are our parents so unreasonable?" said Jasmine. "We've already got cats, so a couple more kittens in our house for a few weeks wouldn't make any difference. I bet they wouldn't even notice them. And your mom works from home, so you'd think she'd be happy to have a beautiful little kitten to keep her company."

"I know," said Tom. "I don't understand them at all."

8
This Is Our Chance

"Do you like it?" Jasmine asked Tom. "We put the tree up earlier than usual because of this dinner party."

"It looks amazing," said Tom. "Your decorations are so nice."

Jasmine turned to the kitten in her arms. "Isn't it pretty, Holly?"

"She loves the lights," said Tom. "Look how she's staring at them."

It was four weeks later, and Holly was eight

weeks old. Mom and Dad were giving a dinner party tonight. Jasmine couldn't remember them ever doing such a thing before, but Mom had decided that they owed several people an invitation and they might as well invite them all at once and get it over with. Although it was still only morning, Mom had already laid the dining table with candles and wineglasses and the antique china that had belonged to Jasmine's grandmother.

"And I know we usually wait until Christmas Eve to decorate the tree," she had said, "but it will be nice to have the house looking festive. And if the tree's up, hopefully everyone will look at that and not the dust."

So they had cut down a tree from the woods yesterday afternoon and had spent the morning decorating it. Holly had been banished from the room after causing havoc by leaping into boxes of decorations, shredding tissue paper, and chasing ornaments around the floor.

While the dinner party was going on, the children were also to be banished, in their case to the living room for pizza and TV, which to Jasmine seemed the better option by far.

"Don't let the cats anywhere near this room from now on, OK?" said Mom, adjusting a place mat by half an inch.

"I won't," said Jasmine. "We just brought Holly down to see the pretty lights."

"Well, pop her back in her playpen and go and fetch the cat basket for those kittens."

Since the kittens were now weaned, Mom had decided it was time to trap, neuter, and return them and their mother to the shed, before the cat became pregnant again. Despite all Jasmine's attempts at persuasion, Mom had remained firm.

"They'll be perfectly happy in the shed," she said. "You can still put food out for them. They'll have a good life as farm cats and they'll help to keep the vermin down."

Over the past few weeks, Jasmine had gradually moved the cat's food and water bowls closer and closer to the toolshed, until finally she had put them in the shed itself. She had also put a cardboard box lined with an old blanket in there so they didn't have to sleep on sacks.

Jasmine had hoped that the cat would become friendly if she was being fed, and then she would be able to play with the kittens and tame them.

But it hadn't worked out that way.

The cat tolerated Jasmine bringing food in, but she hissed and spat if she tried to approach her kittens.

So Jasmine just watched them through the shed window. The kittens jumped onto boxes, scrabbled over sacks, tumbled in and out of flowerpots, and endlessly wrestled one another, rolling over and over on the dusty floor and nipping one another's tails and fur. They tried to play with their mother, too, but she mostly just batted them away with her paw.

"I bet it would only take us a few days to tame them," Jasmine said as they walked to the shed with the cat basket. "We could probably have them tamed by Monday if you'd let us bring them indoors."

Mom pretended she hadn't heard.

The trap for the mother cat was a large cage with a spring door that could be set to snap shut when the cat stepped on a metal plate on the cage floor. It had already been in the shed for a few days with the spring door wedged open. Jasmine had put the food bowl inside it, so the cat had gotten used to walking into the trap for her food. Last night, Mom had set the spring once Jasmine had placed the food bowl inside, and the cat had walked into the trap right away. She hissed and spat at first, but they had put a blanket over the trap to make her feel safe, and she had calmed down after a while.

"I know it doesn't seem nice to trap her," Mom had said, "but she'll be much happier and health-ier in the long run. And we have to catch her the night before, because she'll only walk into the trap for food, and she can't have any food for twelve hours before the operation."

They had blocked up the hole in the shed wall

so the kittens couldn't escape, and Jasmine had removed their food bowl before she went to bed, so that they, too, would have empty stomachs before their operations.

Now, Mom softly opened the door. The cat was sleeping in the trap and the kittens were curled up in their box.

Tom and Jasmine, each holding a small towel, crept toward the sleeping kittens. They caught each other's eyes and then, at the exact same time, they each picked up a kitten, wrapped it snugly in a towel, and held it close to their chests.

"Neatly done, you two," said Mom. "Good work."

Jasmine smiled at the beautiful tabby kitten in her arms. It had blue eyes and thick, fluffy fur. It was meowing but not struggling. She held it against her chest and stroked it gently, up the forehead and down between the ears. "Hello, little one," she said.

The orange kitten was wilder than the tabby. It

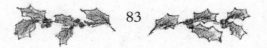

was struggling, hissing, and spitting. Tom held it firmly and stroked its head.

"Look at its eyes," he said. "They're bright green."

"They're amazing," said Jasmine. "Are they boys or girls, Mom?"

Mom took the tabby kitten and examined it. "This one's a girl."

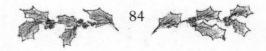

Tom handed her the orange kitten. She held it in the towel as she examined it. "And this one's a boy."

The kitten stopped struggling and fixed his big green eyes on Mom. She looked back at it. "You are very lovely," she said.

Tom and Jasmine glanced at each other. Was Mom weakening?

Mom handed the kitten back to Tom. "All right, put them in the carrier and drape the towels on top."

Her phone rang and she stepped into the garden to answer it. She was on call again this weekend.

With a heavy heart, Jasmine placed the tabby kitten in the plastic cat carrier. Tom did the same with her brother. The kittens meowed and ran to the sides, trying to escape from this strange new prison.

"It's OK," said Jasmine. "You're all safe. And you won't be in there for long."

Mom came back into the shed. "Bad timing, I'm afraid. I've got to go to a calving. I shouldn't be long. Just put the kittens' carrier next to the trap, and I'll take them to the office when I get back. Give them a bowl of water and they'll be fine for an hour or two. Thank goodness Dad's cooking tonight. I'll see you soon."

She hurried off.

Jasmine looked at Tom, her eyes gleaming with excitement.

"This is our chance! I bet we could tame them in a couple of hours. Let's take them inside."

Tom's eyes lit up. Then they clouded over with doubt. "What about your mom?"

Jasmine shrugged. "What can she do? She can only put them outdoors again, and she's doing that already. And this way, we've got one more chance to convince her that we can look after all three of them. Come on. Let's see if these two remember their sister."

In Jasmine's room, Holly was dribbling a

Ping-Pong ball around her playpen. She stopped and ran to the side of the pen when Tom and Jasmine came in. They set the carrier gently on the floor next to her.

"Holly, your sister and brother are in this carrier," said Jasmine. "Do you remember them?"

"Holly must smell completely different now," said Tom. "They won't recognize her scent."

He lifted the towels off the cat carrier. The kittens ran at the sides, trying to find a way out. Tom and Jasmine spoke to them softly, trying to calm them down. Holly shrank back and watched her sister and brother intently from a safe distance.

"They'll be exhausted in a minute," said Jasmine.

Sure enough, after a few minutes the kittens started to calm down. "We should pick them up and handle them," said Tom.

"We need to pick Holly up, too," said Jasmine, "or she'll get jealous. I'll fetch Ella."

Ella was quite happy to be called away from

her books to come and pet a kitten. "You take the tabby," said Jasmine. "She's tamer. I'll take the wild one and Tom can pet Holly. Ella, you open the door, and Tom and I will get the kittens."

They wrapped the kittens in towels as they took them out of the carrier. Tom handed the tabby to Ella and then let Holly out of her playpen. Holly purred as he held her and talked to her. The other two kittens struggled and mewed as Jasmine and Ella stroked them.

"You should call the orange kitten Mistletoe," said Ella, "because his eyes are the color of mistletoe leaves."

"Then the tabby should be Ivy," said Tom.

"Holly, Ivy, and Mistletoe," said Jasmine. "Perfect."

She turned as the door opened. Ben and Manu stood in the doorway. Their eyes lit up as they saw the kittens.

"You brought them in!" said Manu. "Did Mom change her mind?"

"Not exactly," said Jasmine, "but we're going to tame them and then she will."

"We should do that experiment on them," Ben said to Manu.

"Oh, yes," said Manu. "Can we borrow one, Jas?"

Jasmine held Mistletoe closer. "No way are you two coming near these kittens," she said. "What experiment anyway?"

"It's a science experiment we thought up," said

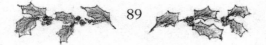

Ben. "You know how everyone says cats always land on their feet?"

"And everyone says toast always lands butter side down," said Manu. "So we thought if we tied a piece of buttered toast to a cat's back and dropped it out of a window, we could see which way up it landed, and then we'd know which rule was stronger."

"If you dare come anywhere near these kittens, Manu," said Jasmine, "I'll tie a piece of toast to your back and throw you out of a window. Then you can see how you like it."

9
What Have You Done with Them?

It wasn't long before all three kittens were fast asleep. Ella brought her homework into Jasmine's room so she could guard them from kidnap attempts while Jasmine and Tom took Sky for a walk.

Mom still wasn't back when they returned. Ella was sitting at Jasmine's desk, surrounded by books, typing on her laptop. But the doors of the carrier and the playpen were wide open, and the kittens were nowhere to be seen.

"Ella," said Jasmine, "where are the kittens?"

"What?" said Ella vaguely, her eyes on the screen.

"Where did you put the kittens?"

"Nowhere. Why?"

"Oh, no," said Tom. "Manu and Ben must have sneaked in and taken them."

Jasmine's face blazed with fury. "They'd better not have!"

Manu's room was empty. Tom and Jasmine raced downstairs. Manu and Ben were sitting on the living-room sofa, watching cartoons.

"Where are the kittens?" asked Jasmine, looking wildly around the room. "Where are they?"

The boys remained glued to the TV. Jasmine grabbed the remote and switched it off. Ben and Manu swung their heads around, their faces the picture of outrage.

"Hey!" shouted Manu. "What are you doing?"

"What have you done with the kittens?" yelled Jasmine.

"They're here somewhere. We were playing with them. Give me the remote."

"But they're not here, are they? What have you done with them?"

"We didn't do anything. They must have gone somewhere else."

"You terrors!" yelled Jasmine. "They're only eight weeks old. Anything could have happened to them!"

Tom was running around the room, lifting up cushions and looking under furniture. Then he turned to Jasmine, looking panic-stricken.

"What if they've gone into the dining room?" he said.

Jasmine stared at him for a second. Then they ran into the hall. The dining room door stood ajar. They pushed it open.

The first thing they saw was Holly and Mistletoe chasing each other around the dining table. As Jasmine ran to grab them, Holly's tail swiped the stem of a wineglass. It crashed against a candlestick and smashed into tiny pieces. Holly leaped off the table in fright and landed on

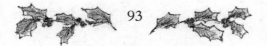 93

Marmite, who was dozing on the carpet.

Marmite sprang up in alarm and tried to jump onto the table, but she misjudged the distance and ended up clinging to the edge of the white tablecloth with her claws. The cloth started slipping off the table, pulling glasses, place mats, and candlesticks with it as Marmite struggled desperately to disentangle her claws from the fabric.

As Tom dashed over to free her, a wineglass rolled off the table and crashed to the floor. Marmite jerked back in shock, finally freed herself, and sprang up into

the Christmas tree. It wobbled and shook. Toffee jumped into the tree after her. They chased each other around the branches, sending ornaments and decorations crashing to the floor. Jasmine and Tom tried to grab the cats, but they climbed up out of reach.

Then Jasmine spotted Mistletoe, perched on the very top branch. As Marmite climbed toward him, Mistletoe leaped from the tree to the bookcase, sending all the Christmas cards toppling to the carpet.

Meanwhile, Holly had discovered a roll of wrapping paper. Pushing at the tube, she quickly managed to unroll the entire three yards. Ivy leaped on the end of the paper as it curled up, biting it and tearing it with her claws.

Toffee and Marmite were both at the top of the tree now. Marmite hissed at Toffee and lashed out with her paw. Jasmine and Tom looked on in helpless horror as Toffee sprang out of the tree and landed on the sideboard, knocking over Mom's vase of flowers. The water spilled onto Holly and Ivy and soaked their roll of wrapping paper. The drenched kittens howled in shock and started running around the room. Toffee shot out into the hall.

The door from the kitchen opened and Dad appeared, holding a bunch of carrots.

"What on *earth* is going on?" he shouted.

Spooked by the yelling, Marmite leaped from the top of the tree. At least, she tried to leap, but her paws got caught in the strand of lights and the force of her jump unbalanced the whole thing.

The tree came crashing down on the dining table, smashing the remaining wineglasses and scattering pine needles and decorations all over the room. Marmite untangled herself with a yowl of terror and fled. All three kittens shot from the room in different directions.

A terrible silence descended on the dining room. The only sound was the drip, drip, drip of water from the overturned vase. Jasmine didn't dare look at her father.

The key turned in the front door. Mom's car keys clattered onto the hall table. Mom appeared in the dining room doorway and her eyes widened in horror.

"What have you done?" she shrieked. "Jasmine Green, what *have* you done?"

When Jasmine confessed that she had brought the kittens in, her parents were angrier than she had ever seen them. They sent Tom off to find the kittens, and then they rounded on her.

"This is *exactly* why we told you not to bring those kittens indoors," said Dad. "You were told again and again, and you completely disobeyed us."

"We were going to tame them," said Jasmine. "It was all Manu's fault. He let them out. We were being responsible."

"Responsible!" shouted Mom. "Responsible? What you did, Jasmine, is the exact opposite of responsible."

"But—" Jasmine began.

"Don't you dare argue back," said Mom. "Look at the state of this place. Every one of those breakages is coming out of your and Manu's allowances. And I was going to clean the bathroom after I'd operated on the cats, and now I'm going to have to clean up this room instead. So you are going to clean the bathroom, and the downstairs one, and they had better be sparkling clean or you'll do them again."

"And then you can peel all the vegetables for dinner," said Dad, "because I won't have time to

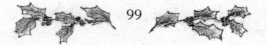

do that along with the chom chom batches. And those two boys can switch off that television and fill up the log baskets. No more television for any of you today. I've got enough jobs to keep you all busy until you go to bed at six o'clock."

"Six o'clock!" said Jasmine.

"You heard me," said Dad.

"And in the morning," said Mom, "you can write out an advertisement for Holly and we'll find her a proper home."

"No!" said Jasmine. "Please, Mom . . ."

"I won't hear another word about it," said Mom. "If you're not responsible enough to listen to instructions, you're certainly not responsible enough to have another cat. We're advertising Holly tomorrow."

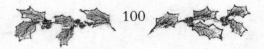

10
You Can't Let Her Go There

The first people who phoned about the advertisement arranged to come and see Holly on Wednesday evening. Two more families were coming on Thursday.

Ivy and Mistletoe were back in the shed with their mother. In her heart of hearts, Jasmine had to admit they seemed happier outdoors. And now that they had been neutered, they should have healthier lives.

But Holly wasn't a feral kitten anymore. She was tame and socialized, and she needed a home.

When the doorbell rang as the family was fin-
ishing dinner on Tuesday, Mom clapped her hand
to her mouth. "Oh, it's those people. I completely
forgot."

"What people?" asked Jasmine.

"I bumped into one of the moms from your
school this morning, and she said her daughter
really wants a kitten, and asked if I could recom-
mend any breeders. So I suggested they come and
look at Holly."

Jasmine stared at her mother in alarm. "What
was her name?"

"Tina Bradley," said Mom, walking to the door.
"I think her daughter's in your class."

Jasmine jumped up from her chair. "Mom, you
can't! She's—"

But Mom was already in the hall. "Jasmine!"
she called. "Go and fetch Holly."

Jasmine stomped upstairs. "Don't worry," she
whispered to Holly as she scooped her out of the
playpen. "There's no way I'm letting you go to her."

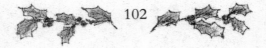

When Jasmine brought Holly into the living room, Bella Bradley and her mom were sitting on the sofa opposite Mom. Bella, who had never spoken nicely to Jasmine in her life, now greeted her as if they were best friends. Then, as her eyes fell on Holly, she opened them very wide and said, "Oh, she's so cute!"

She turned to Mom with a simpering smile. "Could I possibly hold her, Dr. Singh?"

Seething inside, Jasmine handed Holly over.

"Oh, thank you, Jasmine," Bella said sweetly. "Look, Mommy, isn't she the cutest little kitty you ever saw?"

She started talking to Holly in a sickly voice, the kind some people use when talking to babies. Her mother smiled at her fondly.

"Bella adores animals," she said proudly to Jasmine's mom. "She's been so wanting one of her own. And she's an only child, so it's nice for her to have pets, isn't it?"

"Do you have other animals?" asked Mom.

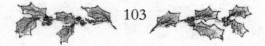

"Just a dog," said Mrs. Bradley, "and he's as good as gold. He won't be any problem with a kitten."

"Is that the dog who killed a nesting duck in my dad's sheep field?" asked Jasmine, trying to keep her voice calm. "Didn't the police come to your house afterward?"

Mrs. Bradley went red. Bella looked up at Jasmine's mom with big, sad eyes.

"That was so, so terrible," she said. "I cried for days about that poor duck, didn't I, Mommy?"

Jasmine opened her mouth to remind Bella that her exact words when she had seen the dead mallard were, "So? It's just a duck." But before she could speak, Bella hurried on.

"I think I was in shock at the time, because it was so awful, but I cried for days afterward, didn't I, Mommy? And it really taught me a lesson. I've never taken Rupert out without a leash since then. And if I see anyone else in a sheep field with a loose dog, I always tell them to put it on a leash. So I might have actually saved the

life of other innocent animals. It would be nice to think I've done something to make up for that terrible day. I'm so, so sorry, Dr. Singh. I still feel really bad about it. And Jasmine was so amazing to save the little duckling, wasn't she?"

Jasmine glanced at Mom. Surely she wasn't going to fall for this?

"Well, that's very nice of you to say," said Mom. "Anyone can make a mistake, and it's great that you've learned from it."

"Thank you, Dr. Singh. That's so kind of you. Oh, listen, Mommy, she's purring! I think she likes me."

"Of course she does, dar-ling," said Mrs. Bradley. "She's such a cute little thing, isn't she?"

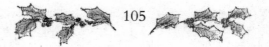

Jasmine looked sadly at Holly. Even she had fallen for Bella's act.

"Would you like her, do you think, sweetie?" asked Mrs. Bradley.

"Oh, yes, please, Mommy. I'd like her more than anything. She's the cutest kitten ever."

Jasmine couldn't bear this. She had to have one last try at saving Holly.

"There is one thing we need to tell you," she said.

"Yes?" said Mrs. Bradley.

"The thing is," Jasmine said, "Holly was rejected by her mother. And that might mean there's something wrong with her. Cats usually reject their kittens for a reason, so even though she seems all right at the moment, there may be a problem with one of her internal organs that hasn't shown up yet."

Mrs. Bradley looked alarmed. Mom laughed.

"Oh, honestly, Jasmine," she said. "That's nonsense and you know it."

"You said it yourself! You said there might be something wrong with her that we don't know about yet. And it wouldn't be fair to give Bella a kitten that isn't healthy."

"I said that when she was two weeks old," said Mom. "She's more than eight weeks old now and I've never seen a healthier kitten."

"We'll definitely take her, then," said Mrs. Bradley. "We'll pick her up next week."

Bella threw an arm around her mother's neck. "Oh, thank you, thank you so much, Mommy! You're the loveliest, kindest mommy in the whole wide world."

Jasmine made a noise as though she was about to be sick. Mom shot her a furious look.

As they were leaving, Bella glanced at Jasmine and said, "I don't really like the name Holly. I think I'm going to give her another name. Would that be all right, Dr. Singh?"

"Of course," said Mom. "You can call her anything you like, once she's your kitten."

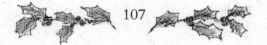

"No," said Jasmine, once Mom had shut the front door. "Just no. I'm not letting Holly go to Bella Bradley."

Mom held up her palms. "I'm not listening, Jasmine. Holly is going and that is that."

"But her dog's a duck murderer! What if he kills Holly? He easily could. She's way smaller than a duck. You can't let her go there, Mom, you just can't."

"Honestly, Jasmine," said Mom, "I've absolutely had enough of your pestering. Those people seemed perfectly nice, and dogs and cats live together quite happily in millions of households."

"But she doesn't even want a kitten! She just wants all the cute accessories. We heard her talking about it at school. She'll get bored with Holly after a few weeks. She won't love her properly. Not like I do."

Mom looked as though she was about to explode.

"OK, OK," said Jasmine. "I know I'm not allowed to keep her. But can't we wait until the other people have come to look at her and then see who'd be the best owner?"

Mom took a deep breath.

"The truth is, Jasmine," she said in the quiet voice that Jasmine hated, "you don't want Holly to go to anyone. You've been determined to keep her ever since you first brought her in. The most perfect family in the world could walk through that door right now and you'd find some reason why they weren't right. Bella might be a bit sickly sweet, but she clearly liked Holly, and I'm sure she'll look after her."

Jasmine opened her mouth again.

"That's enough, Jasmine," said her mother. "I mean it. Holly has found a new home, and I don't want to hear another word from you."

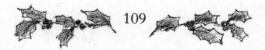

11
A Bit of a Shock

Tom came to the farm on the following Sunday to play with Holly for the last time. Bella was going to pick her up the next day.

"I brought her some new toys," he said, pulling from his backpack a knitted Father Christmas and two silver ornaments. "The ornaments aren't glass, so they won't smash. They can remind her of us."

Holly loved her new toys and spent a happy hour chasing the ornaments and wrestling with Father Christmas.

"I bet Bella won't play with her for long," said Tom.

"No, she'll get bored after a few days like she does with everything," said Jasmine.

"And then Holly will be really lonely," said Tom.

Jasmine glanced at him. He looked sadder than she had ever seen him.

"Maybe she'll be OK," she said, not because she believed it but to try to make Tom feel better. "Some cats like to be left alone."

Tom shook his head. "Not Holly. She likes company."

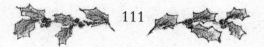

After lunch, they played with Holly until she curled up and fell asleep on Jasmine's sweater. Jasmine put her in her playpen while she and Tom took Sky for a walk and went to see Truffle. When they returned, Tom went upstairs to check on Holly while Jasmine groomed Sky in the mudroom.

The phone rang while Jasmine was washing Sky's food bowl. A couple of minutes later, Mom came out to the mudroom, the phone in her hand. She looked furious.

"That is unbelievable," she said. "What nerve. A complete waste of time."

"What?" said Jasmine.

"Those Bradleys."

"Oh, them," said Jasmine scornfully. "What have they done now?"

"I hate to admit it," said Mom, "but you were right about Bella Bradley all along."

"Of course I was," said Jasmine. "Why, what's happened?"

"That was Tina on the phone. They're not going to take Holly anymore."

Jasmine stared at her. "No way. Really?"

"Really. They've changed their minds."

Jasmine whooped in delight. "Oh, that's amazing! Why did they change their minds?"

"Apparently Bella decided she didn't want a

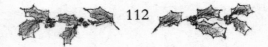

kitten after all. She wants a new phone instead."

Jasmine snorted. "See? I told you what she's like."

Mom sighed. "I know, I should have listened to you. It made me very thankful that you really care about your animals."

Jasmine looked disgusted. "As if I'd ever be like Bella Bradley."

"It's such a nuisance, though," said Mom. "I called the other people who'd inquired about Holly, but they've all found other kittens now, and it's too close to Christmas to re-advertise. We'll have to wait until after New Year's."

"Unless . . ." said Jasmine, giving her mother what she hoped was an irresistibly appealing look.

"Unless what?"

"Well, you did say how good I am at looking after animals. And Holly's so cute and beautiful. You wouldn't really want her to go to another home, would you? You'd miss her, too, I know you would."

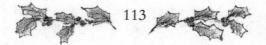

113

Mom hesitated. "Well . . ."

"Please, Mom? Please? For my Christmas present? I'd never get bored with her, you know I wouldn't."

"Well," said Mom, "you have looked after her very well, and she is lovely."

Jasmine held her breath.

Mom smiled. "All right, Jasmine. Holly can be your Christmas present."

Jasmine gasped in delight and threw her arms around her mother. "Oh, thank you, Mom! Thank you so, so much! I'm going to tell Tom. And I'm going to tell Holly she can stay with me forever. Thank you *so* much, Mom."

She ran into the hall. "Tom!" she called. "Come down here! I've got the best news!"

The doorbell rang. Jasmine opened the door. Tom's mom was standing on the step.

"Hello, Mel," said Mom, coming into the hall. "Come in."

"I won't, thank you," said Miss Mel. "I'm afraid I need to take Tom home."

Tom appeared on the stairs with Holly in his arms. "You said I was staying for dinner," he said to Miss Mel. "Why are you so early?"

"Are you all right?" Mom asked her. "You don't look well."

Miss Mel's face contorted as though she was trying not to cry. "It's just . . . we've had a bit of a shock." She swallowed. "It's Richard's mother. Tom's granny."

"What?" said Tom, hurrying to the door. "What's wrong?"

"Oh, Tom," said Miss Mel, bending down and putting her hands on his shoulders. "Tom, I'm so sorry. Granny has died."

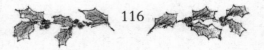

12
An Answer for Everything

Tom came to school as normal during the last week before the holiday, but he wasn't at all like his usual self. He looked really sad all the time, and he barely spoke a word. During class, he seemed very far away, and Jasmine could tell he didn't hear anything the teacher said. When they were supposed to be working, Tom just sat with a pencil in his hand, staring into space.

The worst thing, Jasmine thought, was that the rest of the class was in a state of feverish excitement.

Every afternoon was spent making decorations for the classroom, or holiday cards for their parents, or practicing for the holiday show. Tom joined in all these activities, but Jasmine could tell how sad he was inside, and her heart ached for her friend. It was going to be such a lonely Christmas for him.

On the last day before break, Tom came to the farm for dinner and to drop off his guinea pigs. His family was going to Cornwall the next day for the funeral, and wouldn't be back until Christmas Eve. He and Jasmine took Sky for a walk, fed Truffle, and then played with Holly in Jasmine's room.

"I'm so glad you got to keep her," Tom said. "I couldn't have stood it if Bella had taken her. I would have worried about her all the time."

"Jasmine," called Mom up the stairs, "there's juice and cookies if you want some."

"I'll come and get it," Jasmine called back.

In the kitchen, Miss Mel was talking to Mom.

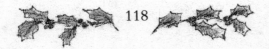

She looked tired and stressed. Jasmine had put the juice and cookies on a tray and was heading out of the room when Miss Mel said, "Jasmine, before you go . . . How does Tom seem to you?"

"Uh . . ." said Jasmine, a little thrown by the question. "Well, he seems sad."

"I wondered if he'd said anything in particular to you. I'm worried about him. He's so unhappy all the time."

"It is very recent," said Mom. "It will take time."

"I know," said Miss Mel, "and I know he's going to be sad for a long time. He loved his granny very much. It's just . . . it feels like it's more than that, somehow. I've always worried about him being lonely, as an only child, but he's never seemed particularly lonely before. But now . . . well, this week, he seems incredibly lonely. And Christmas is going to be so hard for him. He was so looking forward to spending it in Cornwall, and now it will just be the three of us at home together."

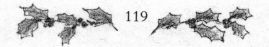

"Why don't you come here for Christmas?" said Mom. "We'd love to have you."

"That's so kind," said Miss Mel, "but I think Richard wants to be at home. I'm just worried about Tom."

"Well, you know he can come here whenever he likes," said Mom. "He's always welcome."

A peal of laughter sounded from upstairs. Miss Mel looked startled.

"Was that Tom?" she said. "Who's he with? I haven't heard him laugh all week."

Suddenly, a strange sensation ran through Jasmine. It was unlike anything she had ever felt before: a curious mixture of excitement, pain, and hope. But despite the confusion of feelings, in that moment, Jasmine knew with absolute clarity what she had to do.

She put the tray back on the table. "Come up and see him," she said to Miss Mel. "But be really quiet."

Looking a bit bemused, Miss Mel followed her up the stairs. Jasmine stopped outside the open door of her bedroom and stepped aside so that Miss Mel had a clear view.

Tom was sprawled on the carpet with his back to them. He had attached a long piece of string to each of the ornaments, and he was pulling them across the carpet in little jerky movements, first one and then the other. Holly was darting between them, pouncing on each in turn as it moved.

Tom let go of the strings and threw the Father Christmas toy high in the air. Holly leaped up to grab it but missed and did a complete backflip before landing on her feet. Tom laughed and scooped her into his arms. "You're the best kitten ever," he said.

As he cuddled her, his face became sad again. Miss Mel put her hand on Jasmine's arm and gestured for her to come downstairs.

She didn't speak until they were in the kitchen. Then she said, "It's funny. I've never been an animal person myself, but Tom really does love animals, doesn't he?"

Mom handed her a mug of tea, which she accepted gratefully. "I almost wish now," Miss Mel said, "that I'd let him have that kitten. But I really don't like cats, what with the scratching and the fleas and the hair they leave everywhere and the dead things they bring in. I just don't know if I could have one in the house."

"Holly only had fleas when we first found her," said Jasmine. "She's really clean now. And we've trained her to use her scratching post instead of furniture. If you groom her regularly, she won't

shed much hair, and you can get her a collar with a bell, so she won't be able to catch mice and birds."

Miss Mel smiled at her. "You have an answer for everything, don't you? But aren't you keeping Holly yourself?"

"I was going to," said Jasmine. "But Tom loves her just as much as I do, and he needs her more. It would make him really happy, I know it would."

"What do you think, Nadia?" asked Miss Mel.

"Well," said Mom, "I think Jasmine might be right, actually. Tom really loves Holly, and she seems to love him, too. She might be just what he needs."

Miss Mel sat silently with her elbows on the table, cradling her mug. Eventually she said, "Let me think about it. I'll talk to Richard tonight. And please, don't say a word to Tom."

13
Merry Christmas, Tom

It was Christmas Eve. Jasmine placed Holly's cat carrier on the back seat of Mom's car and climbed in next to it. She was holding a big shoebox, empty except for Holly's blanket and her woolly Father Christmas. Jasmine had covered the box and lid with Christmas wrapping paper and made some small holes in the sides.

Jasmine hadn't seen Tom since Sunday, although she had spoken to him on the phone from Cornwall. She had also had one very important phone conversation with his mom. Miss Mel knew that Jasmine was coming to their house today, but Tom had no idea.

As they drove up the farm road, an icy white flake landed on the windshield.

"Look!" said Jasmine. "It's snowing!"

More snowflakes splatted against the glass. "It's really snowing!" said Jasmine in delight. "It's going to be a white Christmas!"

"We'll see," said Mom. "It might not stick."

But by the time they arrived at Tom's house, the fields and gardens already looked as though they had been sprinkled with confectioners' sugar.

"It *is* sticking," said Jasmine. "You're going to see snow for the first time, Holly. You're going to have a white Christmas."

She opened the cat carrier, lifted out the little kitten, and kissed the top of her head. "You're not mine anymore," she whispered, "but I'll still see you all the time. And you're going to have a lovely home."

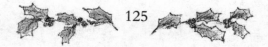

She placed Holly in the shoebox and put the lid on. "It's only for a minute," she reassured her. "You'll be coming out of there very soon."

Mom ruffled Jasmine's hair. "I'm very proud of you, Jas. You're doing a good thing."

"I know," said Jasmine. She went up the walkway with the box in her arms and rang the bell, her mother following behind her.

Inside the house, Miss Mel called, "Tom! Someone's come to see you."

Tom's footsteps sounded on the stairs. "Who is it?"

"Why don't you open the door and see?"

Tom opened the door. His face lit up. "Hi, Jasmine! Hi, Dr. Singh! I didn't know you were coming. I thought we were picking up the guinea pigs later."

"I wanted to surprise you," said Jasmine.

"Come in, both of you," said Miss Mel to Jasmine and her mom.

She led them into the living room, where Tom's dad was putting lights on a Christmas tree.

"We're a bit late with everything this year," he said. "I was hoping you and Tom might decorate the tree, Jasmine, once I've done the lights."

"I'd love to," said Jasmine.

Mom started asking Tom's dad about the funeral and saying how sorry she was, but Miss Mel interrupted. "Shall we let Jasmine give Tom his Christmas present first? Then we can go to the kitchen and I'll make us some tea."

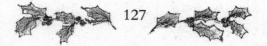

Jasmine's stomach fluttered as she handed the box to Tom. Standing in front of him, all her sadness about giving Holly away disappeared. She felt only excitement as she thought about how happy Tom was going to be.

"Merry Christmas, Tom," she said. "I hope you like it."

"Thank you," said Tom as he took the box. He gave it a little shake.

"Don't do that," said Jasmine in alarm. "It's fragile."

"Fragile?" He looked at Jasmine suspiciously. "It's not a mouse skeleton, is it?"

Jasmine laughed. She and Tom had put the mouse skeleton they had found in the shed into a shoebox and wrapped it up to give to Manu for Christmas.

"Open it and see," she said. "It's not taped up."

Tom set the box on the floor and knelt beside it. He took off the lid. Holly looked up at him and gave a loud meow.

Tom's mouth fell open. He looked up at Jasmine, and then at his parents, with huge, amazed eyes.

Then he said, "Holly? But . . . she's yours. Are you lending her to me?"

Jasmine shook her head. "She's yours now. I

wanted to give her to you, and your parents said I could."

Tom seemed to have lost the power of speech. He stared at Jasmine, then at his parents, then at Holly, then at his parents again.

Eventually he said, in a dazed voice, "Really? Is it true? Is she really mine?"

Jasmine was smiling so hard she couldn't speak; she could only nod. Tom's mom said, "It's true. She's really yours, Tom."

Tom let out a cry of delight. He scooped Holly out of the box and held her to his chest. "Oh, thank you, thank you, thank you!" he said, stroking Holly and staring in amazement at Jasmine and his parents. "Thank you so, so much! I can't believe it."

He cuddled Holly to his chest and she purred loudly. Tom looked up again, his face still amazed.

"She's really mine?" he asked again. "To keep?"

"She's really yours," said his mom. "She's yours to keep. Forever."

As Jasmine headed home that afternoon, she didn't even need the snow to make her feel Christmassy. For the first time in her life, she felt she understood the saying that it is better to give than to receive. No present she received that Christmas could possibly bring her as much pleasure as the happiness she had felt when she had given Holly to Tom.

When she opened her bedroom door, though, and saw the empty space where Holly's playpen had been, she suddenly felt very sad. Holly was gone, and there wouldn't be any more kittens now.

Dad came into the room and put his arm around her.

"Feeling sad?" he asked.

"A bit," said Jasmine.

He squeezed her shoulder. "You did a good thing, Jasmine. You saved Holly's life, and she's gone to a fantastic home. You should be very proud of yourself."

"And I've still got Toffee and Marmite," said Jasmine. "And Button and Truffle and Sky."

"Exactly," said Dad. "And I've been thinking. Sky is just the right age to start proper sheepdog training now. What do you say to rigging up a pen and starting him on some herding practice? We could start the day after Christmas."

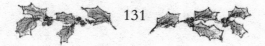

"Oh, yes please!" said Jasmine. "That would be perfect."

As Jasmine was about to hang up her stocking that evening, the phone rang. It was Tom.

"She's sleeping in her playpen next to my bed," he said. "I still can't believe she's really mine. I can't believe she'll still be there when I wake up in the morning."

"I'm so glad you can keep her," said Jasmine. "She's going to love living with you."

"Mom said it was you who persuaded her," said Tom. "She said it all came down to you. Thank you so, so much, Jasmine. Holly is the best present I've ever had."

Turn the page for
an interview with Jasmine and
a sneak peek of the next book in the
JASMINE GREEN RESCUES series!

A Q&A with Jasmine Green

Can I adopt a feral cat?

No, because feral cats have spent their whole lives in the wild, so they behave like wild animals and can't be tamed. They likely won't come near you even if you encourage them. They can look after themselves and live happily outdoors. I wanted to adopt the feral kittens I found after they'd been outside for a while, but in the end my mom persuaded me they'd be happier in the wild (once they'd been neutered).

What should I do if I see a cat outside?

If it won't come near you, it's probably feral and can look after itself. But if it's friendly (maybe after a little encouragement), then it might be a stray. It could also be somebody's pet exploring the neighborhood—or even hoping for a second dinner! But if it seems lost, you could catch it and take it to a vet, who will be able to check for a microchip that would identify the owner. If you can't do that, you could ask around in your neighborhood, put up posters, or ask an adult to share a message with your community online. In the meantime, you could provide food, water, and shelter for the cat. If you can't locate the owner, you can always contact a local animal shelter for advice.

What are good toys for kittens?

Kittens love to play, and they're so much fun to play with. You can buy all kinds of kitten toys, including fancy remote control toys and lasers for your kitten to chase. They love toys with catnip in them, too. But it's also easy to keep kittens amused with things you make yourself. They love chasing a little ball, or an empty spool of thread, or a toy mouse or feather tied to a piece of string. Don't let them play with your fingers or toes, though—that will be very painful once they grow up! They love climbing and hiding, too, so you can have a lot of fun making them a playground of cardboard boxes and tubes.

How many animals do you have now?

I have Toffee and Marmite, my two cats, and Truffle, my enormous pet pig that I rescued when she was a tiny runt. I also have Button, my handsome mallard drake, who lives out on the farm with the chickens. And I have Sky, my lovely rescue collie, who's learning to be a sheepdog. My parents say I have enough pets now, so they made me find another home for Holly. (I disagree, of course—I could easily have more pets!) If you've read this story, you'll know who ended up adopting Holly, and you'll know she couldn't have a better home.

Jasmine Green Rescues

Rescues

A Lamb
Called Lucky

1
Like Baby Dinosaurs

"We have to go in for lunch now, Truffle," said Jasmine, scratching her pet pig behind the ears. "We'll come and see you again this afternoon."

The huge sow gave a contented grunt and lay down under an apple tree. It was hard to believe it now, but Truffle had been a tiny little runt when Jasmine had found her. Jasmine and her best friend, Tom, were planning to run an animal rescue center when they grew up, and Truffle had been their first rescue animal.

In the farmhouse mudroom, Jasmine's cats, Toffee and Marmite, lay curled up in their bed on the work surface. Her collie, Sky, was sleeping on his bed on the floor.

"Look at him," said Jasmine. "That training session tired him out."

Jasmine had found Sky last summer, abandoned and starving. He was a year old now, and Jasmine was training him as a sheepdog.

"We'll be able to give him lots of training now that it's vacation," said Tom.

"Is that you, Jas?" called her mom from the kitchen. "Wash your hands and come in for lunch."

"Coming," called Jasmine.

The rest of her family was already sitting around the kitchen table. Sixteen-year-old Ella had a book propped open in front of her, as usual. Manu, who was six, was wriggling in his chair and chomping noisily on a sandwich, scattering crumbs all around him.

Jasmine handed Tom a bread roll and took one herself. She reached across the table for the cheese.

"Is there any dessert?" asked Manu.

"There's fruit in the bowl," said Mom.

"Didn't you do baking at school yesterday?" asked Dad. "I thought you said you were making cookies."

"That's right, you did," said Mom. "As an Easter present for your family. Are they still in your book bag?"

Manu looked sheepish. "Oh, yes," he said. "I'll get them."

He walked over to the pegs on the wall. From his book bag, he produced a clear plastic box. It contained one small cookie.

"Is that it?" asked Dad. "You made one cookie?"

"Yes," said Manu, studiously avoiding all eye contact.

"Really?" said Mom. "You spent all afternoon making one cookie?"

"Yes."

Everyone's eyes were fixed on Manu as he looked down at the table. After a few seconds, he glanced up at his family. Then he looked down again.

"I might have made more than one," he said.

"Oh?" said Dad. "What happened to the others?"

"They fell on the floor."

"Really?"

"Yes."

"Really?" said Dad. "Would that have been the floor of your stomach?"

Mom tried not to laugh. "I guess you've already

had your dessert, then," she said. "Have some fruit if you're still hungry."

"Should Tom and I check the sheep after lunch?" asked Jasmine.

"That would be great," said Dad. "Then Mom and I can get on with the TB testing."

Jasmine's dad was a farmer and her mom was a vet. That afternoon they were going to be testing the cows for TB. All the cows had to be tested every year to stop the disease from spreading.

"Ben's mom is picking you up at two o'clock," Mom said to Manu. "Ella, can you make sure he's ready, please?"

Ella, deep in her book, didn't respond. Mom repeated the request.

"What?" said Ella vaguely.

Mom sighed. "Manu, go and get your swimming things now, will you? Then you'll be ready to go when Ben gets here."

Ben was Manu's best friend. Like Tom, he spent as much time at the farm as he could, but because

Mom and Dad were working this afternoon, Ben's mom was taking them both swimming.

Dad was reading an article in *Farmers Weekly*. "There's a lot of sheep rustling going on at the moment," he said. "This poor farmer in Yorkshire had his whole flock taken."

"How can anyone steal a whole flock of sheep?" asked Manu.

"Well-trained dogs and a big truck," said Dad.

"Will they take our sheep?"

Dad shook his head. "This is all hundreds of miles away."

"Come on, Tom," said Jasmine, stuffing the last of her roll into her mouth. "Let's go and see the lambs."

Lambing season was Jasmine's favorite time of year at Oak Tree Farm, and the lambing barn was her favorite place. And now, she thought happily, she had two whole weeks with no school and new lambs being born every day.

They could hear the lambs long before they saw them. Their high-pitched bleats and their mothers' low answering calls could be heard all across the farmyard. To a stranger, they might all sound the same. But every one of those lambs could recognize its mother's call amongst the baaing of a hundred other ewes, and every ewe could tell the cry of her own lamb.

The big barn was divided into pens with metal rails. Along the left-hand side were rows of small pens, each containing a single ewe and her lambs. Most of these had only been born yesterday. In the largest pen were the sheep with older lambs. They would be taken out to the field in a few days' time.

Jasmine scanned the animals for any signs of trouble. Sometimes a lamb that had seemed perfectly healthy would suddenly die for no apparent reason. But they all looked well this afternoon.

She turned her attention to the most exciting pen of all, where the sheep still waiting to lamb

were kept. A smile spread across her face as she saw a ewe standing in the middle of the pen with two tiny newborn lambs sucking vigorously from her udder, wiggling their little tails as they fed.

"Look," she said to Tom. "Aren't they gorgeous?"

It never ceased to amaze Jasmine that newborn lambs somehow always knew exactly what they

needed to do. Just a few minutes after they were born, they would heave themselves up on their wobbly legs, stagger to their mother's udder, and start to drink.

Unless there was something wrong, of course. That was why somebody had to check the sheep every few hours. But there was nothing wrong with these two.

Jasmine and Tom scattered fresh straw on the floor and filled up the hay racks and water buckets. When they were finished, Tom said, "Should we go and give Sky another training session?"

They were about to leave the barn when Jasmine glimpsed something bright yellow lying in the straw. She bent down to examine it, and drew in her breath.

"What is it?" asked Tom. He crouched beside her.

"Oh!" he gasped.

The flash of yellow that Jasmine had seen was the edge of a beak. It belonged to a tiny baby bird, sprawled in the straw. And now Jasmine saw another identical baby bird, nearly buried in the straw beside it.

They must have been almost newly hatched, because their eyes were closed and they had no feathers at all, just shiny skin, pink with patches of scaly gray on the wings and head, and a gray line down the back.

You couldn't really call them cute. In fact, they were remarkably ugly. They looked more like baby dinosaurs than birds.

"They must have fallen out of the nest," said Tom. "I can't believe they're still alive."

They watched the birds' tiny chests rise and fall with their heartbeats.

"They won't survive much longer on their own," said Jasmine. "We have to do something to help them."

Which animals have you helped Jasmine rescue?

☐ A Piglet Called Truffle
☐ A Duckling Called Button
☐ A Collie Called Sky
☐ A Kitten Called Holly
☐ A Lamb Called Lucky
☐ A Goat Called Willow

About the Creators

Helen Peters is the author of numerous books for young readers that feature heroic girls saving the day on farms. She grew up on an old-fashioned farm in England, surrounded by family, animals, and mud. Helen Peters lives in London.

Ellie Snowdon is a children's author-illustrator from a tiny village in South Wales. She received her MA in children's book illustration at Cambridge School of Art. Ellie Snowdon lives in Cambridge, England.